future

Don't Hug the Pug

Written by Robin Jacobs
Illustrated by Matthew Hodson

British Library Cataloguing-in-Publication Data.

A CIP record for this book is available from the
British Library.
ISBvN: 978-1-908714-65-7
First published in 2019 by:
Cicada Books Ltd
48 Burghley Road
London, NW5 1UE
www.cicadabooks.co.uk

Printed in Poland

Don't Hug the Pug

Written by Robin Jacobs
Illustrated by Matthew Hodson

cicada

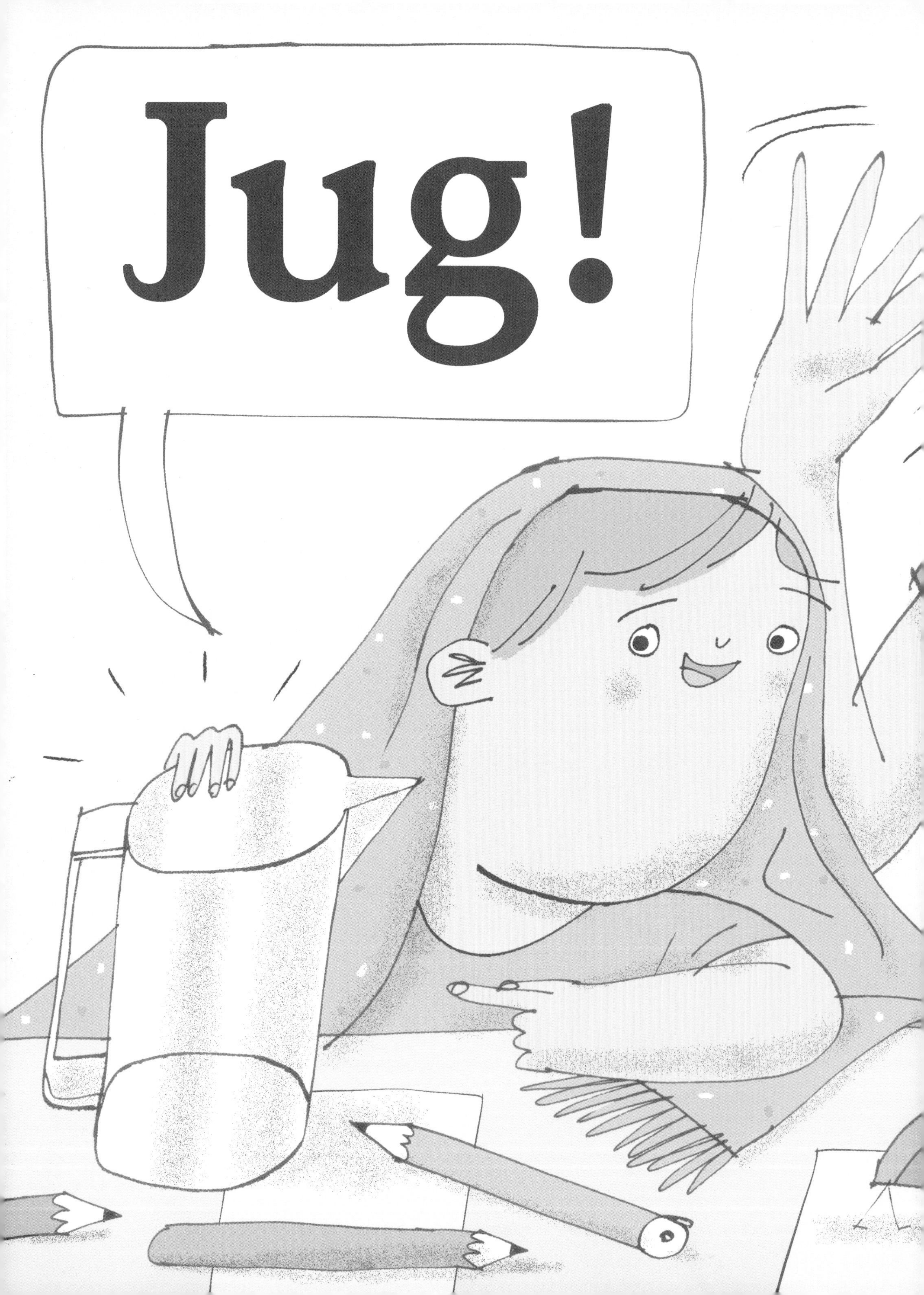
Jug!

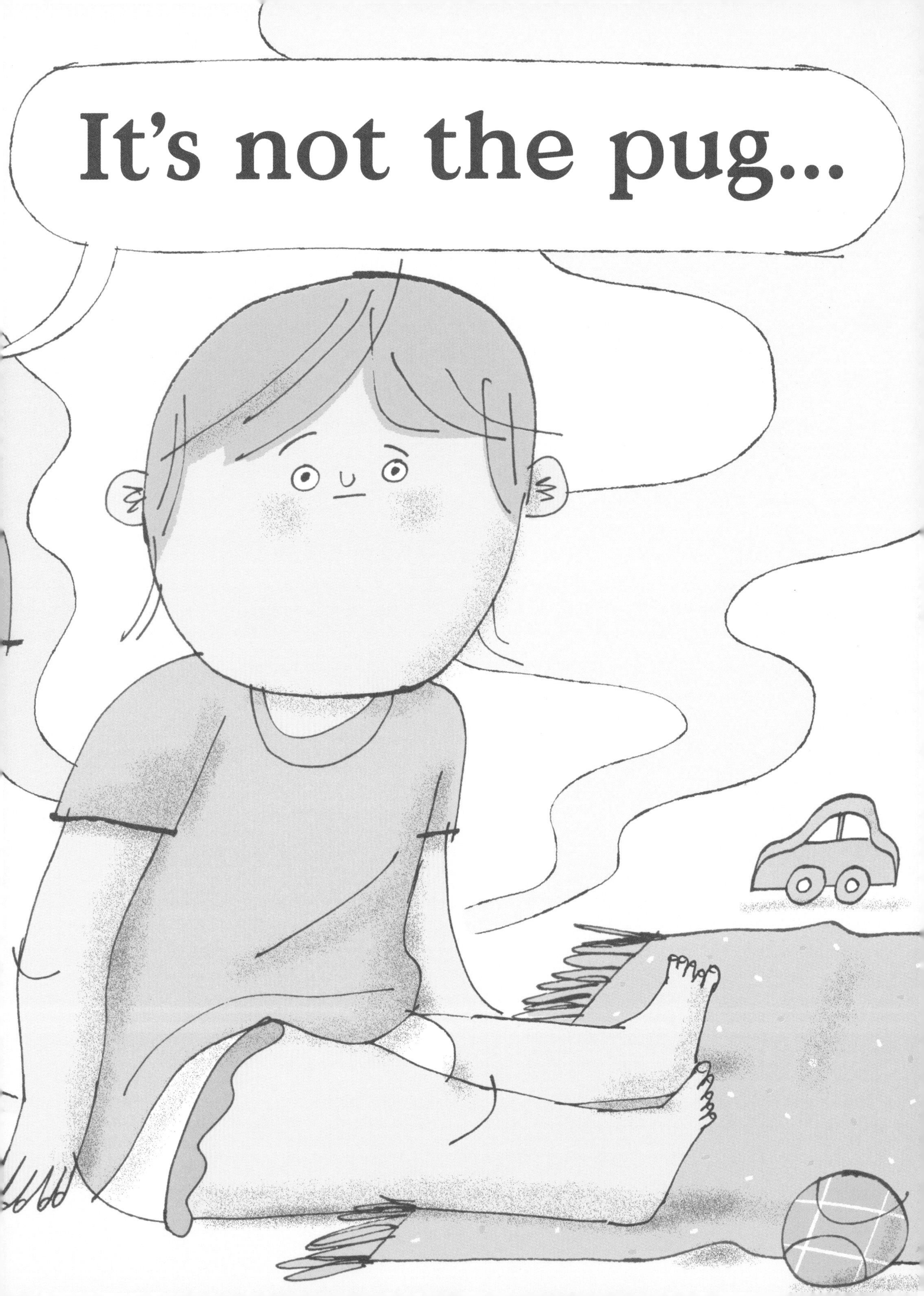
It's not the pug...